Hot Lips Harrison

by Helen Johnson

Illustrated by Gary Andrews

CHAPTER 1

Monday Morning

I looked at Linsey Lee and sighed. Linsey was standing at the bus stop talking to Vicky Smith. Well, actually Vicky Smith was doing all the talking. Linsey was just listening and smiling and nodding her head. I loved the way she listened and smiled and nodded her head. Mind you, I loved everything about Linsey – from her battered trainers to the fringe that got in her eyes. I thought Linsey Lee was fantastic.

But I was dead worried about asking her out. I sighed again.

"I don't know why you don't just ask her," said Gavin.

Gavin's my best mate and he knows *nothing* about girls.

"Look – if you don't ask her, I will," said Gavin. "I'm sure Linsey would be very interested in my rock collection."

When Gavin talks about rock, he doesn't mean loud music. Gavin's rocks are those hard things you find in the ground.

That did it. I couldn't let Linsey be bored to death by Gavin's rocks. I saw the bus coming round the corner at the bottom of the hill. It was now or never.

"Do you want to come to the pictures on Saturday?" I said.

My voice came out all funny and squeaky, and I could feel my ears going red. But at least I'd said it.

I waited for Linsey to start laughing. But she didn't.

She just said, "OK."

OK? I couldn't believe it! "You mean you *will* go out with me?"

Linsey nodded.

"Really?" I said.

She smiled – one of her nicest smiles when her mouth goes up at one side. "Really," she said.

Linsey Lee had said "Yes" to Dean
Harrison.

I felt like jumping up and punching the
air, like they do in football when they've
scored a goal. (But I didn't, of course.)

For the first time in my life I couldn't
think of anything to say. I just stood there
smiling like an idiot.

CHAPTER 2

Monday Afternoon

I smiled like an idiot all day.

I even managed to keep smiling when I got home and saw Kim. And I don't normally smile when I see her.

Kim's my sister and she's horrible. Don't get me wrong – I've got nothing against girls. Some of them are fine. Some of them are even quite normal. (And some, like Linsey for instance, are perfect.) It's just sisters that are a pain.

If you've got a sister, you'll know what I mean. If you haven't, you're lucky.

Kim is the kind of girl that's enough to put you off girls for life. I can't think what Jason (her boyfriend) sees in her. He must need glasses.

Kim was standing by the sink, making herself a fish finger and pickle sandwich. I ignored her. I always do. I got myself some crisps and sat down. One of Kim's magazines was on the table. I started reading it.

Suddenly Kim snapped, "You said you didn't like that song!"

"What song?" I hadn't got a clue what she was on about.

"The one you've been humming for the last two hours!" she said.

Two hours? I hadn't been home two minutes!

Then she started wailing that terrible tune – the one that goes:
Turn the lights down low
You don't have to go.
You don't have to miss me –
Just kiss me.

I **hated** that song. "Shut up – it's horrible!" I said. "Especially when *you're* singing it."

"You started it," said Kim.

How could I have been humming that song and not even noticed? You don't have to miss me – just kiss me! **Kiss!**

I suddenly went hot and cold all over. I might have to kiss Linsey! Not that I didn't want to – I did! I just hadn't thought of it before.

"You've gone all red!" said Kim. "It's a girl, isn't it!" she sneered.

"No, it's not," I lied.

Just then the phone rang. Kim ran off to answer it – it's always somebody for her. Saved by the bell!

Kissing! That was something new to worry about! I mean, I'd never done it before. Not properly, anyway. I'd kissed Grandma and stuff like that, but that didn't count. How did you do it? And when? And would Linsey want me to?

I needed some advice – and fast. But who could I ask about kissing? Kim probably knew all the answers – she's the sort of pain who knows everything. But it would be no good asking her. I could just imagine what she'd say:

"What do *you* need to know about kissing for? Who'd want to kiss *you*?"

Then before you knew it, she'd have told all her friends too:

"Hey – guess what! Dean's thinking of **kissing** somebody!"

Then the whole school would know. No, it was no good asking her.

It would be no good asking Gavin either. He'd just say, "I dunno." That was his answer to everything. The only thing Gavin knew about was rocks, and that wasn't going to be much help when it came to kissing Linsey.

I flicked through the pages of Kim's magazine. What a load of rubbish! *My Dream Date … Hunting for Hunks … Need a new face? Enter our great make-over competition!* Must remember to tell Kim about that one … *Dear Fiona …* The problem page! This could be it! Maybe somebody had written in and asked Fiona about kissing.

I read the whole page. I learned how to dump my boyfriend (which was no use to me). And how to ask somebody out (too late for that). I even knew what to do if a dress fell to bits two days after I bought it. But it seemed as if girls didn't want to know

how to kiss. Maybe they were just born
already knowing.

I turned to my horoscope. My star sign is Leo, the lion, in case you were wondering. Kim says that means I make a lot of noise and belong in a zoo. (She's Scorpio – which you might have guessed. Scorpio is the scorpion – that nasty, spiteful creature with a sting at the end of its tail.) According to Kristal Starr, I was in for a tricky week:

LEO
July 24 – Aug 23

Things are hotting up in your love life.
It's time to bring a new talent to light, but beware of making a fool of yourself. Make sure you know what you are doing before you set out.

It was uncanny! Maybe Kristal Starr really could see into the future. Had she seen a picture of me in her crystal ball trying to kiss Linsey? Was I making a fool of myself? Or had I got a talent for kissing that I didn't know about yet?

Kim came back from the phone. (It was an amazingly short call – must have been a wrong number.) She was in a *really* bad mood now.

"Get your dirty hands off my mag," she said, and snatched it off me.

Dirty hands! They might have looked a bit grubby, but they were clean underneath. Anyway – you ought to see Kim's room! It's a right tip. You could keep a hippo in there for a fortnight and nobody would notice. But I bet the hippo would complain about the mess.

Kim stomped out of the room and stamped upstairs. I heard her door slam. I guessed the phone call wasn't a wrong number after all – it must have been Jason. And they must have had a row. Again. Kim and Jason are always falling out. I just can't understand why Jason ever bothers to fall back in with her again.

CHAPTER 3

Monday Night

I'm a born worrier. I can't help it. I'm one of those people who has nightmares about going to school in pyjamas. I worry about **everything**.

You know how the more you worry about something, the worse it gets? That's how it was when I was worrying about kissing Linsey. I kept thinking of things that could go wrong. I could easily make a fool of myself, like Kristal Starr said. Linsey and I might fall over. She might punch me. I might get hiccups. Or I might not be able to breathe – I might faint. Linsey might go off me and spread lies about me. She might tell everybody I had bad breath. Or maybe I *had* got bad

breath! I tried breathing into my hands to check, but all I could smell was school soap and cheese and onion crisps. That was something else to worry about. (Remind me to buy one of those mint spray things.) We might bump noses or bang teeth. Somebody might see us ... I had a **lot** of worrying to do.

It was dead quiet at tea, with me worrying and Kim being miserable.

"You two are quiet for a change," said Mum. "Is anything wrong?"

"No," said Kim and I together.

"Eat your pizza, then."

"I'm not hungry," I said.

"I'm on a diet," said Kim.

"What's that? The fish-finger-and-pickle-sandwich diet?" I said.

"Oh, shut up!" shouted Kim. Then she burst into tears and ran out of the room.

I saw Mum mouth "Jason trouble" to Dad, then she followed Kim upstairs.

It wasn't fair – nobody asked me about *my* troubles. I couldn't burst into tears and storm out of the room. I just had to sit there with a stiff upper lip. I felt my lip with my finger. It didn't feel very stiff. Would this make a difference when I kissed Linsey?

"Stop frowning, Dean," said Dad. "You'll get a crinkly forehead."

A stiff upper lip **and** a crinkly forehead – all these worries about women were making me old before my time.

I had a terrible nightmare that night. Linsey and I were on a massive football pitch. Linsey was wearing her football kit and boots with huge studs. (Linsey is brilliant at football.) I was wearing my pyjamas. Linsey was dribbling the ball and I kept trying to tackle her. All the crowd were booing me. When I got the ball Linsey pushed me out of the way. I landed nose-first in the mud and got a nose bleed. All the crowd started cheering and doing a Mexican wave. When I woke up there was blood all over my pillow. I really *had* got a nose bleed. I get loads of them. Hope I don't get one when I kiss Linsey. Better remember to take a hankie on Saturday, just in case.

CHAPTER 4

Tuesday Morning

Tuesday was awful. I was so worried I couldn't eat my lunch. I kept looking at all the other kids talking and laughing. None of them looked like they'd got anything to worry about. They probably all knew about kissing.

I looked over at Linsey. She was sitting on the other side of the hall between the Barrett twins. They were both talking at once and Linsey was listening and nodding. I waved and she smiled and waved back. I sighed. I was bound to make a mess of it on Saturday night.

"What's wrong with you?" said Gavin. "Has Linsey changed her mind about going out with you?"

"No! Why?" I said.

"Oh, nothing. It's just that you look dead miserable." Gavin stuck a forkful of chips in his mouth. "I don't know why you're so worried about Saturday night," he said. "She's only a girl."

Only a girl! Saying Linsey was only a girl was like saying that Ryan Giggs was only a footballer! Linsey wasn't like any other girl I knew. She didn't keep flicking her hair back and looking in mirrors. And she didn't talk all the time either.

I started doodling a spider on the back of my hand.

"Gavin? If you didn't know something and you wanted to find out, where would you go?"

"It depends what it was," he said. "Like if it was a maths question, I'd look in Miller's maths book. He always gets his sums right."

Miller is the original swot. He might know all about long division but I bet he knows nothing about kissing.

"How about if it was something else?" I said. "Nothing to do with maths at all?"

"Well, my dad always tells me to go and look in the dictionary."

I went into the library after dinner and looked up "kiss" in the dictionary. It said:

Kiss: To touch or press with the lips.

That was no use to me – I knew that already. Besides, it didn't sound very romantic. I couldn't see Linsey coming over all swoony because I'd pressed her with my lips. It sounded more like ironing than love.

CHAPTER 5

Tuesday Evening

When I got home, there was one of those sloppy black and white films on the telly. I wouldn't normally watch it, but I thought there might be some kissing in it. I might learn something.

The hero was this bloke called Grant. He was about seven feet tall with massive shoulders and a frilly white shirt. The girl was called Mary. She kept fainting all over the place. Right at the end there was a fire and Mary was trapped in the house. Grant rushed right into the flames and up the stairs. Then he found her and carried her out. He didn't get burnt but his shirt got a bit dirty.

The last shot was when Mary opened her eyes. She looked at Grant and said, "Grant," and he said, "Mary." Then she said, "Grant," again, and he said, "Mary." Then just when she was about to say Grant for the third time, he kissed her. I think he was just trying to shut her up.

When the credits rolled, they were still kissing – and Grant was still carrying her! I wondered how Grant was managing to breathe, kiss Mary **and** carry her at the same time.

I knew I wouldn't be carrying Linsey anywhere – she was bigger than me for a start. She'd probably end up carrying me. One thing I did notice about Grant – he had these dazzling white teeth. I might not be able to carry women out of burning buildings, but at least I could clean my teeth. I decided to go and give mine a really good scrub.

I read somewhere that it's supposed to take at least five minutes to clean your teeth properly. Have you ever tried to clean your teeth for five minutes? It feels like ages. I got arm-ache before I was halfway through.

Then Kim started banging on the door telling me to hurry up. She's always doing that. I'm sure she does it on purpose.

"Dean! Hurry up!"

"I'm cleaning my teeth!"

"Why? You're not going to the dentist's, are you?"

That's the sort of remark she thinks is funny. I carried on cleaning my teeth. Two more minutes to go.

"Dean!" Thump, thump, thump. "Come on! I've got dye on my hair. I've got to rinse it off!"

Kim's always dyeing her hair different colours. I don't know why she bothers – she still looks awful.

One more minute.

"It'll go all wrong if you don't let me in!"

Good.

I rinsed my mouth out and dried my face on the towel.

"Dean! Open this door!"

I opened it.

You should have seen Kim's hair! It was bright orange.

Of course, I got the blame. But it was almost worth it.

CHAPTER 6

Wednesday

The next morning Gavin went into the newsagent's to get the latest copy of *Rock World*.

I was waiting near the magazines when something caught my eye. It was this magazine called *Hers!* It had a big red stripe right across the cover. On the stripe it said:

FREE THIS WEEK – TOP TIPS FOR HOT LIPS!

Our pull-out guide tells you everything you ever wanted to know about kissing. Who? How? What? When? and Where? Get Top Tips free with this week's *Hers!* and have the hottest lips in town!

There it was! The answer to all my problems – except one. How on earth could I buy *Hers!* without Gavin seeing?

I went back to the newsagent's after school. There were some kids in there choosing sweets. I picked up this bike magazine and pretended to read it until they'd gone. I had just taken *Hers!* off the shelf when Swotty Miller came in and picked up one of those crossword magazines.

"Hello, Dean," he said.

I nodded at him. I slipped the copy of *Hers!* behind the bike magazine so he wouldn't see it.

The woman at the counter called, "Who's next?"

"After you," said Miller.

"No, it's OK," I said. "You go first."

Miller stepped back. "Please – I insist."

"Come on," said the woman, crossly. "I haven't got all day."

She held out her hand. Miller was

standing between me and the magazine stand. I couldn't put the bike magazine back without him seeing *Hers!* So I handed them both over.

"That'll be three pounds sixty," said the woman.

Nearly two weeks' pocket money for two magazines! And I didn't want either of them!

As soon as I got outside I stuffed the Top Tips guide in my pocket and binned the mags. Then I ran home to do some reading.

CHAPTER 7

Top Tips for Hot Lips

OK – you've done the basics – you've cleaned your teeth and changed your t-shirt. Now it's time for action! Just follow our step by step guide to the perfect kiss:

1) THE LOOK OF LOVE

Look him in the eye and wait till his eyes meet yours. Once you've made eye-contact, don't look away or he'll think you're not interested.

2) TOUCH-DOWN!

Keep looking as your lips meet – then you can close your eyes (if you want to).

3) GENTLY DOES IT

Relax! Snogging's not a wrestling match or a test-your-strength contest. Be gentle with him!

4) OPEN OR SHUT?

There isn't a right way or a wrong way to kiss. Whether you open your mouth or not is up to you – just do what feels right. There's only one person who knows what's right for you – and that's YOU!

5) ENJOY YOURSELF!

Don't waste time worrying about how you're doing – nobody's going to be giving you marks out of ten for style and content. Just focus on the feeling and go with the flow ...

6) PERFECT TIMING

Question – How long should a kiss last?
Answer – As long as you want it to!
Just remember, it's not a marathon. The longest-ever kiss may have lasted over 17 days, but you're not trying to set a new world record. Keep it on the short side – you can always go back for more.

And finally –

7) PRACTISE MAKES PERFECT!

Everything worth doing takes practice, and kissing is no exception. Practise kissing on the back of your hand and get used to the feel of your lips. Better still – find a willing partner to practise with. The longer it takes to learn, the more fun you'll have!

FUN FACTS

❤ Polar bears kiss too ❤ The average kiss lasts 4.6 seconds ❤ A good kiss uses 39 different muscles ❤ Most girls close their eyes, but less than half the lads do – depends what you're looking at, we suppose! ❤ Eskimos don't kiss at all – they rub noses instead!

4.6 seconds? How on earth did they know? Had somebody been going round with a stop-watch? And did that include all those granny-pecking kisses?

I put Top Tips in my top secret hiding place under ... I'd better not say where, or it won't be top secret anymore, will it?

Chapter 8

Wednesday Evening

I was going to keep quiet about my date until the last minute on Saturday. If Mum and Dad knew I was going out with Linsey, Kim would get to know too – and I'd never hear the last of it.

But on Wednesday night Mum said that she and Dad would be going out on Saturday night so we'd have to look after ourselves.

"You're not going to the pictures, are you?" I said. It would be just my luck to be sitting there with Linsey, and have Mum and Dad breathing over my shoulder. I could just imagine Mum tapping me on the arm and telling me not to get choc ice all over my best jeans.

"No," said Mum. "Why? What's on at the pictures?"

"Oh – nothing much," I mumbled. "I just thought I might go, that's all."

"It's that Disney thing for five-year-olds!" said Kim. "Haven't you and Gavin grown out of them yet?"

"I'm not going with Gavin," I mumbled, hoping nobody would hear.

But of course, Kim did.

"I know! It's that **girl!**" she yelled. "You're taking a **girl** to the pictures!"

I felt my ears turning red. I wish they wouldn't do that.

I knew she'd be like this.

"What girl?" said Dad.

"Her name's Linsey," I said.

"Dean pesters her all the time at the bus stop," said Kim.

"I don't pester her. I just talk to her. She's very nice. Unlike **some** people I could mention."

"Oooooh!" said Kim. "Maybe she doesn't have to put up with a brother like **you**."

I glared at her. "Anyway – aren't you going anywhere on Saturday night? What's happened to Jason? You haven't mentioned him for at least three days. Has he dumped you again?"

That shut her up. She stormed out of the room. Again. We could do with revolving doors in our house.

CHAPTER 9

Thursday

When I came out of the bathroom after my teeth-cleaning session the next morning, Mum was waiting out on the landing.

"So you remembered, then?" she said.

"Remembered what?" I said.

"The dentist!" said Mum. "You're going this morning."

It was news to me.

"It's written on the calendar," she said.

I got this horrible feeling. Like the one you get when you turn up for your maths lesson and suddenly remember you've got a test that day.

"You know," said Mum. "He's fitting your brace today."

Sometimes things just can't get any worse.
Even missing double history didn't cheer me up.

✳

Having a brace was awful. How on earth
could Linsey bear to kiss me now? Great – I
was going on a date with the best girl in the
whole school, and I'd got about as much sex
appeal as a rusty coat hanger.

"It's not so bad," said Mum. "You can
hardly tell it's there. At least you won't have
crooked teeth."

"What's wrong with crooked teeth?"
I said. At least, I tried to say that. It sounded
more like, "Wash rong wish cookig teesh?"
It's not easy talking with a mouthful of metal.

That night I couldn't eat my fish and chips
at tea. I had to have soup instead.

"Don't worry. You'll soon get used to it,"
said Mum. "The dentist said it would only
take a couple of days."

"I might have starved to death by then," I
moaned. I probably wouldn't have the
strength to kiss Linsey on Saturday, even if
she did want me to.

"I'll have Dean's pudding," said Kim.

"What happened to your diet?" I said.

"I don't need to diet," said Kim. "Jason
says I'm perfect just the way I am."

Oh, yuk. It was back on again.

I was right in the middle of the kissing
practice that evening when Kim burst into the
room.

"What on earth are you doing?" she said.

"What are you creeping around for?" I said. "You could have given me a heart attack."

"Why were you eating your hand?" she said.

"I wasn't eating it," I said. "I was just ... thinking."

"That makes a change," said Kim.

"Ha, ha. Very funny," I said.

Why were sisters always just where you didn't want them to be?

CHAPTER 10

Friday

I went to school on my bike the next morning – I just couldn't face Linsey yet, with my brace. I couldn't even say her name properly, and I'd been practising all night. It just came out as "Linshee". And I kept slobbering.

There was nothing in Top Tips about kissing with a brace. I could just imagine what it would say though:

Brace Yourself!

Question: Should I kiss someone if I'm wearing a brace?
Answer: No.

I know Gavin isn't the best person in the world at noticing things. He goes round in a daze most of the time. But I felt quite miffed when he still hadn't noticed my brace by lunchtime.

"Have you noticed anything different about me?" I said.

I did this big grin so he was bound to see it.

"Yeah!" said Gavin. "You've got a spot on the end of your nose!"

"What!" I grabbed my spoon and looked at myself in it. I wished I hadn't. My nose looked massive – and the spot looked about as big as a pumpkin! I once worked out (in a very boring maths lesson) that the average life span of a human being was about 25,000 days. Out of 25,000 days, why had my very first spot chosen this one to crop up? I was cursed!

"Actually, I was talking about this," I said, pointing to my teeth.

"What?" said Gavin. Honestly, sometimes I wonder how I put up with him.

"My brace!" I shouted. "You know – this massive metal thing stuck to my teeth!"

"Oh, sorry – I didn't notice," he said.

"How can you not notice?" I said. "It's **obvious!**"

Gavin shrugged. "You can hardly tell it's there," he said. "Anyway, it's not important. Loads of people have them."

"Not important?" I screeched. "For one thing, I can hardly eat. I'm never going to get through this liver." It was like trying to chew a car tyre. It tasted like one too. "And what's Linsey going to make of it?"

"She probably won't notice either," said Gavin. "After all, it's dark in the pictures, isn't it? Can I have your jam tart?"

"Help yourself," I said. I lowered my voice. "Yes, but what about ... you know ..." I looked round to check that nobody was listening.

"What if I kiss her or something?" I whispered.

Gavin shrugged. "I dunno," he said. A hundred bits of pastry sprayed out over the table. "Why? Are you going to?"

I went cross-eyed and looked at the spot. "Probably not," I said.

I began to wonder if there had been any point in reading Top Tips at all. I hadn't even seen Linsey since Monday – maybe she was avoiding me. And the way I looked, she would probably scream if I tried to get near her. If she wasn't going to let me kiss her, there wasn't much point in me being an expert at it.

I felt really fed up when I got home. I scrubbed out the cat's milk saucer and thought about Saturday night. It was going to be a disaster. Maybe I'd just have to give up the idea of girls altogether. Maybe I'd just be a monk. I stuck the saucer on my head to see what I'd look like with one of those bald patches. I was just looking at myself in the

mirror when Kim walked in. She didn't even say anything this time. She just shook her head and walked out again.

CHAPTER 11

Saturday

By six o'clock I was a nervous wreck. I read through Top Tips for the last time – I just about knew it off by heart. But somehow, knowing what to do didn't seem to help much – I'd still got to do it. I was beginning to wish I'd never asked Linsey out in the first place.

I went upstairs and locked myself in the bathroom. I had a shower. I cleaned my teeth (and brace) until they were sparkling. I plastered my sticking-up-hair down with a big blob of Kim's hair gel.

Then I dabbed some of Kim's *Stop That Spot!* on the end of my nose. It didn't help much – it just made the spot orange instead of red.

My best jeans were at the bottom of the linen basket – smelling of Dad's socks. I had to wear my old jeans with the dodgy zip. And the only socks I could find were my yellow ones with Postman Pat on.

"Don't worry," said Mum. "You look very nice."

When your Mum says your clothes look nice, you **know** you're in trouble.

CHAPTER 12

The Date

Linsey was waiting for me in the foyer. She was standing in front of this poster of Sylvester Stallone looking tough. (I mean Sylvester Stallone was looking tough – not Linsey!) Linsey looked great. She looked a bit like Mary in that film – sort of shiny. The only trouble was, I didn't look anything like Grant. Heroes never have braces, spots and yellow socks. (Especially not with Postman Pat on them.)

"Hi!" I said. I tried not to open my mouth too much so she wouldn't see the brace.

"Hello," said Linsey.

She looked so nice I could have kissed her right there and then. But there were too many people watching. I thought I'd wait until we got inside.

It was dark and cosy inside the cinema. I looked around to make sure there wasn't anybody I knew. Now was my chance. I leaned towards her ...

"Hasn't it been awful weather this week?" she said.

"Mmmmm," I said. I gazed deep into her brown and green eyes.

"The weatherman said it would brighten up but it hasn't," she said.

"No," I murmured. I moved a bit closer. She was bound to look at me soon. We'd make eye contact, and then ...

"Maybe it will be sunnier tomorrow," she said.

She was beginning to sound like a weather forecast. I was staring so hard, my eyes started to sting. I had to blink.

"Are you all right?" she said.

"Yeah. Just got something in my eye," I said.

Then the film started.

I decided to wait till afterwards. Anyway, it would be more romantic outside.

I can't remember much about the film. I was too busy trying to remember what to do. Relax, make eye contact, take a deep breath, eyes open, eyes closed ... Or was it lips touch, then eyes closed? I wished I'd written the list on my arm. I wondered if Linsey would notice if I got the book out and had a quick check?

When the film finished, we went outside and stood on the steps. It had stopped raining. The stars were out.

"See! I told you it would clear up, didn't I?" said Linsey.

Yes – this was definitely the right place! I moved up a step so I was a bit taller than her. She looked up at me. I did my best, warm, sexy smile (something else I'd been practising all week.) Our eyes met ...

"You can hardly notice your brace at all!" said Linsey.

It turned out Gavin had told her. Linsey said she'd asked Gavin why I wasn't at school on Thursday and he'd told her about the brace.

"Gavin's really nice, isn't he?" she said. "He was telling me all about his rock collection. It was very interesting. I've got this lump of flint at home my dad says might have been a dagger. And Gavin says ..."

She went on and on about Gavin and rocks all the way home. I'd never heard Linsey talk so much. She'd always been so quiet before. I couldn't get a word in, let alone a kiss.

I felt the copy of Top Tips in my pocket. It had all been a waste of time. I might as well have let Gavin ask her out in the first place.

When we got to Linsey's gate, she went quiet. She stared at the pavement. "Thanks for asking me out," she said.

"That's OK," I said. I gazed at her eyes as hard as I could, but she still wouldn't look at me.

"Well," she said.

"Well," I said.

"I'd better be going in," she said, looking at her shoes.

I nodded. She was avoiding my gaze. She didn't want me to kiss her. I might as well give up.

"OK," I said. "See you Monday."

Linsey opened the gate and took her front door key out of her pocket. She looked lovely standing there. The light coming through the front door made her hair shine like a halo.

I sighed again. "Bye!"

I turned to go. She tapped me on the shoulder. I looked round.

Before I had a chance to shut my eyes or anything, Linsey gave me a great big smacker right on the mouth! I think it was a bit harder than she meant (about gale force 9 which can cause serious damage to braces). And it was nowhere near 4.6 seconds, and I wasn't relaxed at all – but it was **great**!

Then Linsey waved to me and went indoors, I stood on the pavement in a daze. My heart was pounding and my lips felt a bit bruised. And my foot was throbbing like mad where she'd trodden on it. But it was the best kiss I'd ever had!

When I turned to go, I trod on something. It looked like Top Tips. It must have slipped out of my pocket – good job Linsey didn't see it!

I picked it up – but it wasn't mine. The
cover was a different colour.

I smiled and slipped it in my pocket. Fancy
Linsey worrying about a silly thing like that!